# MIRROR, MIRROR

---

AN ADDICTIVE SUSPENSEFUL PSYCHOLOGICAL THRILLER

SERENA SINCLAIR

# CONTENTS

# 1

## THE QUIET CAGE

The city outside my window was a blur of movement and noise, but here, in this aging apartment building, time seemed to slow down, almost suffocate me. I could hear the distant hum of traffic, the occasional blare of a horn, but it felt like it was coming from another world, one I no longer belonged to. I leaned against the cracked windowsill, tracing the distorted reflections in the glass. The smudges and streaks made everything outside look warped, as if the city itself was twisted, just like my life.

My apartment was a mess. Unfinished canvases leaned against the walls, accusing me with every brushstroke I had abandoned. Paints and brushes were scattered across the floor, mingling with crumpled sketches and empty coffee cups. The dishes in the sink had been piling up for days, a monument to my inability to get anything right lately. I knew I should clean up, but every time I thought about it, the weight of everything I hadn't done, everything I couldn't do, pressed down on me, pinning me in place.

I sighed and turned away from the window. This place was supposed to be my sanctuary, but now it felt more like a cage. The walls seemed to close in a little more every day, the dim light barely filtering through the drawn curtains, casting long shadows that made the room feel even smaller.

I used to believe that moving to the city would change everything. I thought I'd find inspiration here, in the hustle and grind, that I'd finally prove to everyone—especially myself—that I was good enough. But instead, I felt like I was fading, my dreams slipping away like paint washed off a canvas, leaving behind nothing but a dull, lifeless surface.

As I wandered through my apartment, I caught a glimpse of myself in the mirror above the sink. I barely recognized the woman staring back at me. My hair was a tangled mess, dark circles etched under my eyes from too many sleepless nights. I hadn't picked up a brush in weeks, and it showed—

not just in the state of my work, but in the way I carried myself. The spark I used to have, the drive to create, was gone. I felt like a ghost, haunting a life I couldn't escape.

The sound of footsteps in the hallway jolted me out of my thoughts. They were slow, deliberate, echoing through the paper-thin walls. I held my breath, listening as they passed by my door and continued down the corridor. I didn't know why, but something about them made my skin crawl. This building was old, and noises like that were common, but today, they seemed different. There was something off, something that made my heart race and my stomach twist.

Shaking my head, I tried to push the feeling away. I was being ridiculous. It was just someone going about their business, nothing more. But still, the unease lingered, like a shadow that wouldn't leave me alone.

I decided I needed to get out, if only to clear my head. I grabbed my coat and keys, slipping out the door as quietly as I could. The hallway was just as dim as my apartment, the wallpaper peeling in places, revealing patches of cracked plaster underneath. The overhead lights flickered, casting erratic shadows that danced across the walls. I made my way to the elevator, the ancient thing groaning as I pressed the button. It arrived with a shudder, the doors creaking open like they hadn't been oiled in years.

As I stepped inside, I couldn't shake the feeling that something was wrong. I had always hated this elevator, with its creaky floor and the way it seemed to shudder with every floor it ascended. But today, it felt worse. It felt like a coffin, like I was trapping myself in this tiny metal box with no escape. My fingers hovered over the buttons, almost reconsidering, but I forced myself to press the ground floor.

The ride down was excruciatingly slow, every jolt and groan of the elevator making my heart beat faster. I stared at the worn-out panel in front of me, trying to distract myself, but the numbers seemed to change at a snail's pace. By the time the doors finally opened, I was practically running to get out.

The lobby was almost as depressing as the rest of the building, with its faded carpet and dim lighting. I nodded at the doorman, who barely glanced up from his newspaper as I stepped outside. The cold air hit me like a slap in the face, waking me up, clearing my mind a little.

I wandered down the street, not really caring where I was going, just needing to move. The city was alive around me, people rushing by, cars honking, life happening. But I felt detached from it all, like I was watching it through a fog. My feet carried me through the familiar streets, past the cafes and shops I had once loved, but now felt like they belonged to someone else.

Eventually, I found myself standing in front of a gallery. I didn't remember how I got there, but it didn't matter. The windows were filled with vibrant paintings, each one bursting with color and life. I felt a pang of envy as I stared at them, the kind of art I used to dream of creating but had never quite achieved. It was the kind of work that demanded attention, that made you feel something deep inside.

I stepped closer to the glass, drawn in by one piece in particular. It was a portrait, striking and raw, capturing a sense of vulnerability that was almost painful to look at. As I stared at it, I felt a strange mix of emotions—admiration, jealousy, and something else I couldn't quite name. I wanted to know the artist, to understand how they had captured something so real, so powerful.

But then, out of the corner of my eye, I noticed something that made me freeze. A reflection in the glass, just behind me. I turned quickly, but there was no one there. Just the empty street and the shadows cast by the streetlights. I looked back at the reflection in the glass, my heart still pounding. But it was gone, as if it had never been there at all.

I shook my head, laughing nervously at myself. I was just tired, stressed out. My mind was playing tricks on me. But even as I tried to convince myself of that, I couldn't shake the feeling that something was watching me, just out of sight.

I needed to get back home.

## 2

## THREADS OF INFLUENCE

I avoided the laundry room as much as I could. The flickering fluorescent lights, the musty smell of detergent that never quite masked the damp odor of the building, the endless cycle of monotonous noise—it all made me uneasy. But it was late, and I had run out of clean clothes. There was no avoiding it tonight.

I bundled up my laundry, hoping I wouldn't run into anyone. The hallways were eerily quiet as I made my way downstairs, the silence broken only by the creak of the floorboards under my feet. When I pushed open the door to the laundry room, I was relieved to see it empty. I quickly claimed a machine, tossing in my clothes and dumping in a capful of detergent. The machine rumbled to life, filling the room with the comforting white noise of washing.

I leaned against the counter, letting the repetitive hum dull my thoughts. It was easy to lose time down here, where the world outside felt distant, almost unreal. But I couldn't shake the feeling of being watched, that same prickling sensation I'd had in front of the gallery. I tried to ignore it, telling myself it was just nerves, when the door suddenly creaked open behind me.

I turned, and that's when I saw her.

She walked in like she owned the place, her movements fluid and confident. She wasn't much older than me, maybe early thirties, but there was something ageless about her. Her hair was dark, perfectly styled, and her clothes—an effortlessly chic ensemble of a fitted leather jacket over a vibrant dress—made my own worn-out jeans and faded hoodie seem even more pitiful. She had an aura of someone who was always in control, someone who knew exactly who they were and what they wanted. It was the kind of self-assurance I'd always envied.

"Hey," she said, her voice smooth and warm, like

she was greeting an old friend. She flashed me a smile that didn't quite reach her eyes.

"Hi," I managed to reply, suddenly feeling awkward. I shifted, trying to make myself seem smaller, less noticeable.

She crossed the room and started loading a machine next to mine. As she moved, I couldn't help but notice the little details—the way her hands moved with a kind of practiced grace, the subtle scent of her perfume that filled the air around her. Everything about her was polished, put-together, the exact opposite of me.

"I'm Sylvie," she said, glancing at me with a curious look.

"Mia," I responded, trying to match her casual tone, though my heart was starting to race for reasons I couldn't quite explain.

"You're new here, right?" she asked, shutting the washer door with a soft thud. "I've been in the building for a while, but I haven't seen you around."

"Yeah, I moved in a few months ago," I said, feeling suddenly self-conscious under her gaze. It was like she was sizing me up, trying to figure me out in that brief moment.

She smiled again, and this time it seemed a bit more genuine. "It's a nice building," she said, though there was a strange edge to her voice, like she didn't quite believe her own words. "If you don't mind the quirks."

"Quirks?" I asked, curious despite myself.

"Oh, you know," she said with a dismissive wave. "The flickering lights, the creaky floors, the way the walls seem to listen in on your conversations." She laughed, a soft, lilting sound, but I couldn't tell if she was joking.

I forced a smile, though her words sent a shiver down my spine. "Yeah, I've noticed."

"There used to be someone in your apartment before you," Sylvie said, leaning casually against the counter. "A woman. She was… different." She tilted her head slightly, as if considering her next words carefully. "Didn't last long here."

"Really?" I asked, trying to keep my voice steady, but the unease was starting to build in the pit of my stomach. There was something unsettling about the way she said it, like she knew more than she was letting on.

"Yeah, but I'm sure you'll be fine," she said, her tone suddenly light again. "People come and go. It's just the way it is."

I nodded, unsure of what to say. The conversation was taking on a strange, almost surreal quality, like I was missing some crucial piece of information. But before I could dwell on it, Sylvie turned her attention back to her laundry, her demeanor shifting as if the previous exchange had never happened.

"So, what do you do, Mia?" she asked, her voice casual once more.

"I'm an artist," I said, feeling a familiar pang of inadequacy as I spoke the words. The truth was, I hadn't painted anything worthwhile in weeks, but admitting that felt like exposing too much.

Her eyes lit up with interest. "An artist? That's wonderful. What kind of work do you do?"

"Mostly painting," I said, trying not to sound too hesitant. "But I've been, um, experimenting lately."

"Experimentation is good," she said with a knowing nod. "It's how we grow, how we push our boundaries." There was something in her tone, a kind of intensity, that made me feel like she was talking about more than just art.

"Yeah, I guess," I replied, still trying to grasp the undercurrents of the conversation.

"Maybe you'll show me your work sometime," Sylvie said, and the way she looked at me made it seem less like a suggestion and more like a statement. A part of me wanted to say no, to keep that part of myself hidden, but another part of me —the part that longed for validation, for connection —wanted to say yes.

"Maybe," I said, my voice softer than I intended.

Sylvie smiled, a slow, satisfied smile that made my skin prickle with a mix of excitement and something else—something I couldn't quite name but that left me feeling both drawn to her and wary at the same time.

"Well, I'd better let you get back to it," she said, stepping away from the machine. "But I'm sure we'll be seeing more of each other."

"Yeah, sure," I replied, watching as she gathered her things and headed for the door. Just before she left, she paused, turning back to me with an inscrutable expression.

"Be careful, Mia," she said softly, her eyes locking onto mine. "This building has a way of getting under your skin."

And then she was gone, leaving me standing alone in the laundry room, my mind buzzing with questions. I replayed the conversation in my head, trying to decipher the meaning behind her words, but it was like trying to catch smoke with my bare hands—no matter how hard I tried, it kept slipping away.

As I waited for the washing machine to finish, I couldn't shake the feeling that something had shifted, that this encounter with Sylvie was the beginning of something I couldn't yet understand. I was intrigued by her, yes, but also unsettled, as if I had just glimpsed the edge of a precipice and wasn't sure whether to step back or lean forward.

That night, back in my apartment, her words echoed in my mind: *This building has a way of getting under your skin.* I didn't know what she meant by that, not yet, but I had the uneasy sense that I was about to find out.

**3**

---

# THE MIRAGE OF CONNECTION

It started with small things. A casual invitation from Sylvie to join her at an art exhibit she thought I'd like, the kind of event I usually avoided because I felt out of place among people who seemed to have it all figured out. But Sylvie made it sound different, exciting. She was magnetic like that, pulling me into her orbit without even trying.

The gallery was in one of those old, converted warehouses downtown, the kind of place that dripped with authenticity and creative energy. As soon as we walked in, I felt the familiar pang of inadequacy that came with being surrounded by so much raw talent. The walls were lined with bold, provocative pieces that seemed to pulse with life, each one a stark reminder of everything I wasn't.

But Sylvie glided through the space with an effortless confidence, pointing out pieces she found interesting, pausing to chat with the artists as if she'd known them for years. I followed her, trying to absorb some of her energy, to let it drown out the self-doubt that was gnawing at my insides.

"This one's intriguing, don't you think?" Sylvie said, stopping in front of a large abstract painting that was all sharp angles and vibrant colors.

"It's… intense," I replied, struggling to find the right words.

Sylvie nodded, a small smile playing on her lips. "It's fearless. The artist didn't hold back, didn't let anything stifle their expression. That's what makes it powerful."

I nodded, but her words hit me like a punch to the gut. I couldn't remember the last time I'd painted something that felt fearless. Lately, everything I created felt safe, restrained, like I was too scared to let myself really go. It was like I was afraid of what might come out if I did.

Sylvie must have noticed the shift in my expression, because she touched my arm lightly, a reassuring gesture. "You have it in you, Mia. I can tell. You just need to stop second-guessing yourself."

Her words were meant to be encouraging, but they only deepened the pit in my stomach. I wanted to believe her, to think that I could somehow break free of whatever was holding me back. But the more I tried, the more I felt like I was slipping away from myself.

Over the next few weeks, Sylvie and I spent more time together. She had this way of making everything seem easy, of turning even the most mundane moments into something special. We'd sit in her apartment, drinking wine and talking late into the night, sharing stories that were equal parts intimate and revealing. She had a way of drawing things out of me, things I hadn't shared with anyone, and in those moments, I felt a strange mix of vulnerability and exhilaration.

But there was always an edge to our conversations, a subtle undercurrent that I couldn't quite put my finger on. Sylvie would offer advice on my work, her words always laced with a hint of something that made me question whether she was being helpful or critical.

"You should experiment with darker tones," she suggested one evening as we looked over some of my sketches. "Your work is beautiful, Mia, but it could be... deeper. More honest."

"Deeper?" I echoed, trying to hide the sting her words had left. "What do you mean?"

She tilted her head, considering her response. "It's like you're holding back, afraid to really tap into what you're feeling. Don't be afraid to explore those darker emotions. That's where the truth lies."

I nodded, trying to take her advice to heart, but her words echoed in my mind long after she left. Was I holding back? And if I was, what was I so afraid of? The more I thought about it, the more I felt like I was losing touch with who I was, like the lines between me and the person Sylvie wanted me to be were starting to blur.

It didn't stop there. I started to notice how much I was beginning to mirror her, in ways that felt almost unconscious. I found myself drawn to the kinds of clothes she wore—sleek, modern pieces that exuded a confidence I didn't feel but desperately wanted. I started to incorporate some of her suggestions into my art, experimenting with darker, more abstract themes that felt foreign to me but seemed to resonate with her.

At first, I told myself it was all part of the process, that I was just evolving as an artist, but deep down, I knew something was off. The more I tried to become the person Sylvie seemed to see in me, the more I felt like I was drifting away from the person I used to be.

One afternoon, as we sat in a café near the gallery, Sylvie studied me with those sharp, knowing eyes of hers. I had just shown her a new piece I'd been working on, something that felt different from anything I'd done before—darker, more intense, exactly what she'd been pushing me toward.

"It's good," she said, her voice carefully measured. "But it's still missing something."

"What do you mean?" I asked, a familiar knot forming in my chest.

She shrugged, taking a sip of her coffee. "It's hard to explain. There's still a hesitation in your work, a sense that you're not fully committing to it."

I frowned, her words settling over me like a weight. "I don't know what else I can do," I admitted, my voice barely above a whisper.

Sylvie smiled, but it didn't reach her eyes. "You just need to dig a little deeper, Mia. Don't be afraid to lose yourself in it."

Lose myself. The phrase lingered in my mind long after we parted ways. Wasn't that what I was already doing? Losing myself?

In the days that followed, I became more and more aware of the subtle ways Sylvie was influencing me, shaping me. It was as if I was clay in her hands, and she was molding me into something I wasn't sure I wanted to become. But even as that realization began to take root, I couldn't bring myself to pull away. There was something about her, something intoxicating, that made me want to stay close, even if it meant losing parts of myself in the process.

The more time we spent together, the more I found myself questioning my own instincts, my own desires. Was I really becoming a better artist, or was I just becoming a different one—one that fit into Sylvie's vision? And why did I care so much about what she thought?

It was like I was caught in a web, each strand woven tighter with every interaction, every piece of advice that felt like a subtle dig at my inadequacies. I started to dread our meetings even as I craved them, a strange mix of fear and fascination that kept pulling me back to her.

Late at night, lying in bed, I would replay our conversations, dissecting every word, every look, trying to understand the hold she had over me. But the more I tried to untangle it, the more trapped I felt. My thoughts circled back to that first conversation in the laundry room, to the way she'd looked at me, the way she'd said, *This building has a way of getting under your skin.*

I didn't know if it was the building or Sylvie herself, but something was definitely getting under my skin, and I didn't know how to stop it.

**4**

———

# FRACTURED REFLECTIONS

The first time it happened, I convinced myself it was just fatigue. I'd been pushing myself too hard, staying up late to work on new pieces, trying to reach the depths Sylvie kept urging me to explore. But exhaustion only explained so much.

It was early evening, the sun sinking low and casting long shadows across the walls of my apartment. I was standing in front of a half-finished canvas, my brush hovering uncertainly over the surface. The colors had turned muddy, the image unclear, as if my hand no longer knew what it was trying to create. Frustrated, I turned away, rubbing my eyes in an attempt to clear the fog in my head.

That's when I heard it—a faint whisper, barely audible, like a breath of air slipping through the cracks in the walls. I froze, straining to listen, but the sound had already vanished. My heart pounded in my chest as I scanned the room, half expecting to see someone standing there, but I was alone. Just me and the shadows.

"It's nothing," I muttered to myself, trying to shake off the creeping unease. But even as I said it, I knew it wasn't nothing. There was something wrong with this place, something that I couldn't quite put my finger on.

The days that followed blurred together, a haze of sleepless nights and restless days. The whispers became more frequent, always just on the edge of hearing, too faint to make out but loud enough to set my nerves on edge. I started hearing them in the hallway too, little snippets of conversation that stopped the moment I got close, leaving me standing there, staring at empty space.

It wasn't just the whispers. My reflection in the windows began to warp, too. At first, it was subtle— a slight distortion, a twist in the glass that made my face look off. But as the days wore on, it got worse. I'd catch glimpses of myself that didn't quite match, my features stretching into something unrecognizable, something… wrong.

I knew I should talk to someone, maybe even Sylvie, but the idea of reaching out made my stomach turn. What would I say? That I was hearing things? Seeing things? That the building was somehow getting inside my head? I could already hear her voice in my mind, telling me I was overreacting, that I just needed to push through it, dig deeper.

But it didn't feel like digging deeper. It felt like sinking, like I was slowly being pulled under by something dark and heavy, something I couldn't escape.

The nightmares started soon after. They were vivid, more real than anything I'd ever experienced. In them, I was always back in the apartment, but it was different—darker, suffocating. The walls would close in on me, the shadows lengthening and twisting into shapes that reached out, trying to pull me in. I'd hear the whispers there too, but they were louder, more insistent, like they were trying to tell me something, but I couldn't understand the words.

Waking up was no relief. The lines between sleep and wakefulness began to blur, and I'd find myself standing in front of the mirror, staring at a reflection that wasn't mine, wondering if I was still dreaming. But it felt too real to be a dream, too solid, too terrifying.

I started avoiding my neighbors, slipping in and out of the building when I knew no one would be around. Even the thought of running into them filled me with dread. What if they saw it too? The way my reflection had started to change, the way the shadows seemed to cling to me? Or worse— what if they didn't see it, and I was losing my mind?

There were days when I couldn't bring myself to leave the apartment at all, when the walls felt like they were closing in on me, and the only thing that kept me tethered to reality was the familiar clutter of my space. But even that started to change. My canvases began to pile up, unfinished and abandoned, the colors on them darkening on their own, like the shadows had seeped into the paint. I didn't remember painting some of them at all, but there they were—images that felt foreign and terrifying, like they'd been created by someone else entirely.

My phone buzzed one afternoon, jolting me out of a daze. It was a message from Sylvie, asking if I wanted to come over. I stared at the screen for a long time, my finger hovering over the reply button. I wanted to say no, to tell her I wasn't feeling well, but I couldn't bring myself to do it. A part of me still craved her approval, her validation, even as another part of me—one that was growing louder by the day—warned me to stay away.

I found myself standing outside her door a few minutes later, my heart racing. I hadn't even realized I'd left my apartment, hadn't registered the walk over. I raised my hand to knock, but before I could, the door swung open, and there she was, smiling at me like nothing was wrong.

"Mia, I'm so glad you came," she said, her voice warm and inviting. "I was starting to worry about you."

I wanted to tell her everything, to spill out the confusion and fear that had been building inside me, but when I opened my mouth, the words got tangled up in my throat. All I could manage was a weak smile and a nod.

She led me inside, and I couldn't help but notice how perfect her apartment was, how every detail was meticulously curated. It was like stepping into a different world, one that was bright and controlled, the exact opposite of the chaos in my own space.

"Sit down, relax," she said, gesturing to the plush couch. "You look like you've been burning the candle at both ends."

I sat down, the cushion sinking under my weight, and for a moment, I thought I might disappear into it, swallowed up by the softness. I felt small here, insignificant, like a piece of furniture in a room that didn't belong to me.

"I've been… working," I said, my voice sounding distant, even to my own ears.

"Good," she replied, her eyes sparkling with interest. "I knew you had it in you."

There was something in the way she said it, something that made me want to scream. But I couldn't. Instead, I nodded again, trying to ignore the way the room seemed to be tilting slightly, like the ground was shifting beneath my feet.

Sylvie sat down across from me, her gaze steady and unnerving. "You're changing, Mia," she said softly. "I can see it in your work, in the way you carry yourself. You're finally letting go of all that doubt, all those things that were holding you back."

I wanted to believe her, I really did. But the images from my nightmares flashed in my mind, the distorted reflections, the twisted shadows, and I felt a cold sweat break out across my skin.

"What if… what if I don't like what I'm becoming?" I blurted out, the words tumbling out before I could stop them.

Sylvie's smile didn't waver, but there was a glint in her eyes that made my stomach turn. "Change is never easy," she said, her tone almost soothing. "But it's necessary. Sometimes we have to shed our old selves to become something new, something better."

Her words echoed in my head, bouncing around like a mantra I couldn't escape. *Something new, something better.* But better for who? For me, or for her?

I left her apartment feeling more lost than ever, the edges of reality fraying as I walked down the hallway back to my place. The whispers were louder now, filling the empty spaces between my thoughts, and I couldn't tell if they were coming from the walls or from inside my own head.

When I finally reached my door, I hesitated, the key trembling in my hand. The urge to run, to escape this building, this life, was overwhelming, but I didn't know where to go. The world outside felt just as alien, just as suffocating, and the thought of facing it alone made my chest tighten with fear.

I stepped inside, closing the door behind me, and

for a moment, everything was quiet. But then I caught a glimpse of my reflection in the window, and my breath hitched in my throat.

The face staring back at me wasn't mine. It was twisted, contorted, the features warped beyond recognition. I stumbled back, my hand flying to my mouth to stifle the scream that was rising in my throat. But the reflection didn't move, didn't change. It stayed there, mocking me, reminding me of the person I was becoming—someone I didn't know, someone I didn't want to be.

I tore the curtains closed, shutting out the distorted image, and collapsed onto the floor, my head in my hands. I couldn't tell what was real anymore, couldn't trust my own eyes, my own mind.

All I knew was that the whispers were getting louder, the shadows darker, and the person staring back at me in the glass wasn't me. It was someone else, someone I was terrified of becoming. And I didn't know how to stop it.

5

———

## THE PAINTED TRAP

It was raining that night, a relentless downpour that hammered against the windows and filled the apartment with a steady, rhythmic pounding. I had been holed up inside all day, trying to drown out the whispers that had grown more persistent, more insistent, but nothing was working. My head felt like it was splitting open, and I couldn't stop thinking about the distorted reflection I had seen, the twisted version of myself that had stared back from the window. I knew I needed to get out, to clear my head, but there was nowhere to go, no place that felt safe anymore.

That was when my phone buzzed. It was a message from Sylvie.

*Come over. I want to show you something.*

I stared at the words for a long time, my heart racing in my chest. Every instinct told me to ignore it, to stay away, but the pull was too strong. Despite everything, despite the growing fear gnawing at me, I needed to see her, needed to understand what was happening to me. Maybe she had the answers I was too afraid to confront on my own.

By the time I reached her apartment, the rain had soaked through my coat, and I was shivering, though I wasn't sure if it was from the cold or something else. Sylvie opened the door before I could knock, as if she had been waiting for me, anticipating my arrival. She smiled, that same enigmatic smile that always seemed to hold more than it let on, and stepped aside to let me in.

"I'm glad you came," she said, her voice soft and warm, but there was something in her eyes that set me on edge. "I've been thinking a lot about you lately, Mia."

I forced a smile, trying to ignore the unease curling in my stomach. "What did you want to show me?"

She didn't answer right away, just turned and walked deeper into the apartment, expecting me to follow. I hesitated, the urge to leave nearly overwhelming, but I couldn't. Not yet. I needed to know.

Sylvie led me down a hallway I hadn't been down before, to a door at the end that was slightly ajar. She pushed it open, revealing a room I hadn't known existed. It was small, almost claustrophobic, with no windows and walls lined with shelves. At first glance, it looked like an art studio, with canvases stacked against the walls and jars of paint and brushes scattered across the floor, but there was something off about it, something that made my skin crawl.

"I wanted to show you my private collection," Sylvie said, her voice almost reverent. "The pieces that mean the most to me."

I stepped inside, my breath catching in my throat as I took in the room. The paintings were unlike anything I had ever seen before. They were dark, twisted, full of sharp angles and distorted figures, each one more unsettling than the last. There was a violence to them, a rawness that made me recoil, but I couldn't look away. It was like they were pulling me in, forcing me to confront something I didn't want to see.

"This... this is your work?" I asked, my voice trembling.

"Some of it," she said, her eyes never leaving the paintings. "But not all. Some of these pieces belonged to others. People who lived here before you."

The air left my lungs in a rush, my pulse quickening as her words sank in. "Before me?" I repeated, my voice barely above a whisper.

Sylvie nodded, moving to stand in front of one of the larger canvases. It depicted a figure trapped in a swirling mass of shadow, their face contorted in pain, their body twisted in impossible angles. It was horrifying, and yet... there was something familiar about it.

"They were like you, Mia," Sylvie continued, her tone almost tender. "Artists. Creatives. People searching for something, trying to find themselves. But they got lost along the way."

A cold, clammy fear gripped my chest as I looked around the room again, this time noticing the small details I had missed before—the initials scrawled in the corners of some of the paintings, the old, faded photographs tucked into the frames, each one showing faces I didn't recognize. People who had lived in the building, people who had come before me.

"What happened to them?" I asked, my voice barely audible.

Sylvie's gaze shifted to me, her eyes gleaming with a strange intensity. "They couldn't handle it. The pressure. The need to create, to be more. They lost themselves in it, and in the end, they became a part of my collection."

I staggered back, my mind reeling as the pieces began to fall into place. The whispers in the hallways, the strange distortions in the windows, the nightmares, the way Sylvie had been pushing me to go deeper, to lose myself in my work. It all made a twisted kind of sense now.

Sylvie hadn't been helping me. She had been grooming me, shaping me into something she could control, something she could own. And I had walked right into it, blind to the truth until it was too late.

"No," I whispered, shaking my head as if I could shake off the realization. "No, this isn't... You can't..."

"I can," Sylvie said softly, taking a step toward me. "And I have. You're almost there, Mia. Almost ready to be part of something greater."

Panic surged through me, my breath coming in shallow, rapid gasps. I needed to get out, needed to escape before I became another one of Sylvie's lost souls, another forgotten artist trapped in her twisted gallery. I turned to run, but the room spun around me, the walls closing in, the paintings seeming to loom larger, their grotesque images searing into my mind.

"You're not going anywhere," Sylvie's voice cut through the chaos, calm and assured. "You're mine now, Mia. Just like they were."

Her words echoed in my head, and for a moment, I felt myself slipping, the edges of my consciousness fraying as reality twisted around me. But then something inside me snapped, a deep, primal urge to survive pushing through the fog of fear and confusion.

"No," I said, louder this time, my voice steadier than I felt. "I won't let you do this to me."

Sylvie's smile faded, replaced by something cold, something dangerous. "You don't have a choice."

I backed toward the door, my eyes never leaving hers. "Maybe not," I said, my hand fumbling for the doorknob. "But I'm not going to be part of your collection. Not now. Not ever."

I wrenched the door open and bolted down the hallway, the sound of Sylvie's voice chasing after me, filled with an icy calm that was more terrifying than any scream.

"You can't escape what's inside you, Mia. You're already becoming what you fear."

Her words followed me as I fled her apartment, the rain pounding against my face as I stumbled out into the night. My thoughts were a tangled mess, my mind racing with fear and anger and a bone-deep horror that I couldn't shake.

Sylvie was right about one thing—I was changing. But I wasn't going to let her control it. I wasn't going to let her take what was left of me.

As I ran through the rain, the shadows seemed to close in, the city warping around me in a dizzying blur. I didn't know where I was going, didn't care, as long as it was away from her, away from the building, away from everything that had turned my life into a nightmare.

But no matter how far I ran, I couldn't escape the feeling that something had shifted, that something inside me had snapped. And as I looked back at the towering silhouette of the apartment building, shrouded in rain and darkness, I knew one thing for certain.

Nothing would ever be the same again.

**6**

---

# DESCENT INTO DARKNESS

I couldn't sleep anymore. Every time I closed my eyes, she was there, lurking in the shadows of my mind. Sylvie's voice would weave through my thoughts, soft and insistent, telling me things I didn't want to hear, things I couldn't escape. Her words echoed in my head, twisting my dreams into nightmares, and when I woke up, drenched in sweat, the room would feel too small, too dark, like the walls were closing in on me.

It was happening more often now, the lines between waking and sleeping blurring until I couldn't tell what was real and what was just another fragment of my crumbling mind. The whispers had grown louder, more distinct, and sometimes, I swore I could hear them coming from the walls themselves, seeping through the cracks like a living thing.

I tried to fight it, to push her out of my head, but the harder I fought, the deeper she seemed to dig in. The apartment, once my sanctuary, had become a prison, and no matter where I turned, I felt her presence there, watching, waiting.

Days slipped by without me noticing. I lost track of time, the hours bleeding into one another until everything felt like one long, endless day. The canvases in my apartment gathered dust, the paints dried out, untouched. My brushes sat abandoned, forgotten. I couldn't bring myself to pick them up. Every time I tried, my hands would start to shake, and all I could see were those grotesque images in Sylvie's secret room, the twisted figures, the faces of the lost, staring back at me.

It wasn't just the art that was slipping away. I started avoiding people, too. At first, it was just the residents in the building—those familiar faces I'd pass in the hallways, the ones who'd offer a polite nod or a murmured greeting. But now, when I saw them, my heart would race with suspicion. I'd feel their eyes on me, too long, too intense, like they knew something I didn't. Like they were in on it.

Mrs. Latham, the elderly woman from two floors down, used to smile at me every morning when she went out for her walk. But now, when I saw her in the hallway, I could only think about what Sylvie had said—how the others had come before me, how they'd all been drawn in, shaped, and destroyed. I wondered if Mrs. Latham knew, if she had seen them go, one by one, slipping away into the shadows.

One morning, when she smiled at me, I just stared back, my mind racing with dark possibilities. Was she smiling because she knew what was happening to me? Because she had seen it all before? I forced myself to return her smile, but it felt like a grimace, and I saw her expression falter, a flicker of something—fear? Concern?—crossing her face before she hurried on.

After that, I started taking the stairs instead of the elevator, ducking out of sight whenever I heard footsteps approaching. I couldn't face them, any of them. Every glance felt like an accusation, every smile a taunt, reminding me that I was losing it, that I was already too far gone.

But the worst part was when I started seeing her outside the apartment. I'd catch glimpses of Sylvie out of the corner of my eye—just a flash of dark hair, a glint of light off her leather jacket—but when I turned to look, she'd be gone. I knew it wasn't real, that it was just my mind playing tricks on me, but that didn't make it any less terrifying.

Sometimes, I'd hear her voice, too, soft and distant, like she was standing just behind me, whispering in my ear. She'd say my name, over and over, until I was sure she was right there, only to turn and find the room empty.

I became convinced that she was everywhere, watching me, waiting for me to break. And the more I thought about it, the more I began to suspect that everyone in the building was involved, that they were all part of her plan to push me over the edge. It was like they were all in on some sick game, watching me unravel, enjoying the show.

The paranoia grew until I couldn't leave my apartment without feeling eyes on me, judging, assessing. I began to suspect that they could hear my thoughts, that my mind was no longer my own. The idea that Sylvie had somehow wormed her way inside, taken control, left me with a constant sense of dread that gnawed at my insides.

The paintings on the walls seemed to warp and twist when I wasn't looking, their colors darkening, their shapes distorting into grotesque forms that mirrored the nightmares that plagued my sleep. I couldn't tell if they were real or if it was just another hallucination, but the sight of them filled me with a deep, bone-chilling terror. I started covering them with sheets, turning them to face the wall, anything to keep from seeing them, but I could still feel their presence, lurking, waiting.

And then, one night, as I was lying in bed, the room dark and silent around me, I heard her voice again. But this time, it was different. Closer. More insistent.

"Mia…"

I sat up, my heart hammering in my chest, my breath coming in short, ragged gasps. The voice was clearer than it had ever been, and it was coming from right outside my door.

"Mia, let me in…"

I scrambled out of bed, backing away from the door as the voice grew louder, more demanding. My back hit the wall, and I slid down, pulling my knees to my chest, trying to block out the sound.

"Mia…"

I clamped my hands over my ears, squeezing my eyes shut, but the voice only grew louder, echoing in my head, filling every corner of my mind.

"Let me in, Mia…"

"No!" I screamed, my voice hoarse and desperate. "Leave me alone!"

But the voice didn't stop. It kept calling my name, over and over, until I thought I would go mad from the sound of it. I felt like I was drowning, suffocating under the weight of her words, her presence. I couldn't breathe, couldn't think, couldn't escape.

And then, as suddenly as it had started, it stopped.

The silence that followed was deafening, pressing in on me from all sides. I stayed there, huddled against the wall, shaking uncontrollably, waiting for the voice to return, but it didn't. All I could hear was the sound of my own ragged breathing, the thud of my heart pounding in my ears.

When I finally opened my eyes, the room was empty. But the air was thick with her presence, like she had been there all along, watching me, feeding off my fear.

I don't know how long I stayed like that, curled up on the floor, too terrified to move, too exhausted to care. But eventually, the numbness set in, a cold, dead feeling that spread through my body, dulling the edges of my fear.

I was losing it. I knew that now. I was slipping away, bit by bit, until there would be nothing left of me, nothing but the twisted, broken thing Sylvie had created. The realization should have filled me with terror, but instead, it brought a strange, twisted sense of relief. At least then, I wouldn't have to fight anymore. At least then, it would all be over.

But even as that thought took hold, another part of me—some small, stubborn part that refused to give in—fought against it, clawing its way to the surface. I couldn't let her win. I couldn't let her take everything from me, not when I still had some small piece of myself left.

But I didn't know how to fight her. I didn't know how to stop the descent.

All I knew was that if I stayed here, if I kept letting her into my mind, it would be the end of me. I had to get out. I had to escape, before there was nothing left to save.

7

———

## SHATTERED ILLUSIONS

I don't remember deciding to go to Sylvie's apartment. One moment, I was lying in bed, staring at the ceiling, the next, I was standing outside her door, my hand raised to knock. My heart pounded so hard I could feel it in my throat, but my mind was strangely clear, focused. This was it—the moment everything had been building toward. I wasn't sure what would happen, but I knew that I couldn't go on like this, teetering on the edge of madness.

I knocked, and the sound echoed in the hallway, unnervingly loud. For a moment, nothing happened, and I almost turned to leave, but then the door swung open, and there she was, standing in front of me like she had been expecting me all along.

"Mia," Sylvie said, her voice smooth, almost soothing. "I've been waiting for you."

"Of course you have," I muttered, stepping inside without waiting for her to invite me. The apartment was just as perfect as always, every detail meticulously curated, but now, it felt suffocating, like the walls were closing in on me. "We need to talk."

She closed the door behind me, her expression calm, unruffled. "I agree."

I turned to face her, my hands trembling with a mix of anger and fear. "What did you do to me?" The words came out harsher than I intended, but I didn't care. I was beyond caring. "What the hell have you been doing to me?"

Sylvie didn't flinch. Instead, she smiled—a small, knowing smile that made my skin crawl. "I haven't done anything to you, Mia. You did this to yourself."

"Bullshit!" I snapped, my voice rising with the desperation I had been trying to keep at bay. "You've been in my head, twisting everything, making me see things, hear things—"

"I didn't make you do anything," she interrupted,

her tone still maddeningly calm. "I simply helped you see what was already there."

I shook my head, backing away from her, the room spinning around me. "No. No, you've been manipulating me from the start. All those little suggestions, those criticisms, pushing me to be more like you… You wanted to break me, didn't you? To turn me into something else, something that you could control."

Sylvie sighed, as if I was a child throwing a tantrum, and the condescension in her eyes made my blood boil. "Mia, you were already broken when I found you. I just… helped you realize it."

"Helped me?" I echoed, my voice trembling with rage. "You destroyed me."

"No, Mia," she said, stepping closer, her voice dropping to a whisper. "I freed you."

Her words hung in the air, heavy with a truth I didn't want to accept. I had been manipulated, yes, but had I also allowed it to happen? Had I wanted it, on some level, needed it? The thought made me sick to my stomach, but it was impossible to ignore.

"What are you talking about?" I demanded, my voice wavering. "Freed me from what?"

"From the lies you've been telling yourself," she said, her eyes gleaming with that same intensity that had drawn me in from the beginning. "From the false identity you clung to so desperately. You were so afraid of failing, of being seen for who you really are, that you buried yourself under layers of doubt and self-deception. I just helped you strip those layers away."

"No," I whispered, shaking my head. "No, that's not true."

"Isn't it?" Sylvie challenged, her gaze piercing through me. "Why did you come to me, Mia? Why did you let me in? Because deep down, you knew you needed to change. You knew that the person you were pretending to be wasn't real. And you were right—because the real you, the one who's been clawing to get out, is so much more powerful than you ever let yourself believe."

I wanted to deny it, to scream at her that she was wrong, that I was still the same person I had always been. But the words wouldn't come. Because deep down, I knew she was right. I had been afraid— afraid of failing, of not being good enough, of being seen as a fraud. I had let those fears define me, control me, until I didn't even recognize myself anymore.

But that didn't mean I had to let her win.

"You manipulated me," I said, my voice stronger now, fueled by the anger that was still burning inside me. "You twisted everything I was into something you could control, something that served your sick, twisted purposes."

Sylvie's expression darkened, and for the first time, I saw something cold and dangerous in her eyes. "Control?" she echoed, her voice low and menacing. "Is that what you think this is about? Control?"

I took a step back, suddenly aware of how close she had gotten. "Isn't it?"

Her smile returned, but it was colder now, more predatory. "You still don't understand, do you? This was never about control, Mia. This was about creation. I saw something in you, something raw and powerful, and I wanted to help you bring it out. But you fought me every step of the way, clinging to your old, pathetic self, too scared to let go."

"Because I didn't want to become you!" I shouted, the words tearing out of me with all the force of the realization that had been building inside me. "I didn't want to lose myself, to become some twisted version of you!"

Sylvie laughed, a sharp, bitter sound that echoed off the walls. "You think you can escape what you've already become? You're already lost, Mia. The person you were is gone. I didn't destroy you— I transformed you. And now, you're exactly where you were meant to be."

Her words hit me like a physical blow, and for a moment, I couldn't breathe. But then something snapped inside me, a final thread of resistance that refused to break.

"No," I said, my voice cold and clear. "I'm not lost. Not yet."

I moved before I could second-guess myself, grabbing the nearest object—a heavy vase—and swinging it at Sylvie with all the strength I could muster. She barely had time to react before the vase connected with her shoulder, sending her staggering back with a gasp of pain.

But I wasn't done. Years of fear, anger, and self-loathing boiled to the surface, driving me forward. I lunged at her, knocking her to the ground. The vase shattered between us, a spray of shards cutting into my skin, but I barely felt it. My vision narrowed, focusing on Sylvie's face, twisted with shock and fury.

"You think you can just twist people into whatever you want them to be?" I screamed, pinning her down with all my weight. "You think you can just play with people's lives and get away with it?"

"Mia—" Sylvie gasped, trying to push me off, but I was stronger, fueled by a desperation that had turned to rage.

"Look at what you've done to me!" I shouted, shaking her. "Look at what you've turned me into!"

Sylvie struggled beneath me, her nails digging into my arms, but I barely noticed the pain. All I could see was her face, the face that had haunted me for so long, the face that had promised salvation but had only delivered destruction.

"You were nothing before I found you!" Sylvie hissed, her voice full of venom. "You would have wasted away in that pathetic little apartment, drowning in your own mediocrity! I gave you purpose!"

"Purpose?" I spat, leaning in close enough that our faces were inches apart. "You took everything from me. Everything."

"And what did you have to lose?" she shot back, her eyes blazing with fury. "Your life was meaningless before I came along. I gave you power, I gave you meaning, and this is how you repay me?"

"You don't own me," I snarled, tightening my grip on her. "I'm not yours."

For a moment, we were locked in a struggle, our breaths mingling, our faces twisted with rage. But then, something shifted in Sylvie's eyes—something dark, something that made my blood run cold.

"You're wrong," she whispered, her voice a low, deadly hiss. "You've been mine from the moment we met. And you always will be."

And then, with a sudden, brutal strength, she pushed me off her, sending me sprawling to the floor. I tried to scramble to my feet, but Sylvie was already on me, her hands closing around my throat.

The world spun around me as she squeezed, her grip like iron. My vision darkened, and for a moment, I thought it was over, that she had won. But then, through the haze, I saw it—a glint of glass on the floor, a shard from the shattered vase.

With the last of my strength, I reached for it, my fingers closing around the sharp edge. I brought it up in a desperate arc, slashing at Sylvie's arm. She cried out, her grip loosening just enough for me to shove her off and roll away.

Gasping for air, I scrambled to my feet, the shard still clutched in my hand, slick with blood—hers, mine, I couldn't tell. Sylvie was on her knees, clutching her arm, her eyes wide with a mix of shock and something that looked almost like fear. Blood seeped between her fingers, staining the floor in dark, spreading pools. For a moment, the sight of her like that, vulnerable and hurt, almost made me hesitate. Almost.

But then she looked up at me, and the fear in her eyes was gone, replaced by something far more dangerous—pure, unadulterated rage.

"You think this changes anything?" she spat, her voice trembling with fury. "You can't escape what you've become, Mia. You can't escape *me*."

Her words sent a shiver down my spine, but I gripped the shard tighter, refusing to let her see my fear. "Maybe I can't escape what you've done to me," I said, my voice shaking with emotion, "but I can still stop you."

Sylvie struggled to her feet, her gaze never leaving

mine. "You're too weak," she sneered. "You've always been too weak to fight back."

"Maybe," I admitted, taking a step closer, the shard of glass still poised between us. "But I'm not the same person I was when this started. You made sure of that."

She took a step back, her eyes narrowing as she realized what I intended to do. "You wouldn't dare."

I took another step forward, my hand trembling but resolute. "You're wrong, Sylvie. You pushed me too far."

She laughed, but there was a tremor of uncertainty in her voice. "You're nothing without me. If you kill me, you'll lose everything I've given you—every bit of strength, every ounce of power."

"I don't want your power," I said, my voice steady now, the resolve in my chest hardening. "I just want my life back."

Sylvie's eyes widened as she saw the determination in mine, and for the first time, I saw her falter. "You can't—"

But I didn't let her finish. With a cry that came from somewhere deep inside, I lunged forward, driving the shard of glass into her side. She gasped, her hands flying to the wound, but I didn't stop. I twisted the glass, tears streaming down my face as I did what I had to do.

She staggered back, her hands clawing at me, at the air, but there was no strength left in her. With a final, desperate gasp, Sylvie crumpled to the floor, her body convulsing once before going still.

I stood there, breathing hard, staring down at her. The room was eerily silent, the only sound the ragged gasps of my own breath. My hands were covered in blood, my mind numb with the horror of what I'd done. But beneath the shock, there was something else—a strange, overwhelming sense of relief.

It was over.

The woman who had haunted my dreams, twisted my thoughts, and tried to break me was finally gone. I'd won. But as I stood there, staring down at her lifeless body, I realized that victory had come at a cost.

Sylvie was right. I wasn't the same person anymore. I had crossed a line I could never uncross, done things I could never undo. And now, I had to live with the consequences.

I dropped the shard of glass, suddenly sick to my stomach. It clattered to the floor, echoing in the silence, and I stumbled back, away from the body, away from the blood. I turned, half-blind with tears, and fled the apartment, my heart pounding with a mixture of horror and grief.

I didn't stop running until I reached the street, the cold night air hitting me like a slap in the face. I leaned against the building, gasping for breath, my mind a whirlwind of emotion.

What had I done?

I had saved myself, yes, but at what cost? Sylvie was dead, and I was the one who had killed her. No matter what she had done, no matter how she had manipulated me, I had taken a life. The weight of that realization crushed me, and I sank to the ground, sobbing uncontrollably.

But even as the tears fell, even as the guilt and grief tore through me, there was a small, stubborn part of me that whispered that it had been necessary. That I had no choice.

Sylvie had tried to destroy me, but in the end, I had refused to let her win. I had fought back, and I had survived. And now, as I sat there, trembling in the dark, I realized that I was finally free.

But at what cost? The question haunted me as I forced myself to stand, my legs shaking beneath me. I looked up at the apartment building, the place that had been both my sanctuary and my prison, and I knew that I could never go back.

Not after what I had done. Not after what I had become.

I turned away, wiping the tears from my face, and walked into the night, leaving the building—and the person I had been—behind me. I didn't know where I was going, didn't know what the future held, but for the first time in what felt like forever, I was free to find out.

And that, I realized, was the only victory that mattered.

# 8

## ECHOES OF THE FALL

The world outside felt different—quieter, emptier. The city that had once been a constant hum in the background was now muffled, as if the noise had receded along with the chaos that had consumed me. I wandered the streets for hours after leaving Sylvie's apartment, my mind numb, my body moving on autopilot. I didn't know where I was going, and I didn't care. All I knew was that I couldn't go back. Not yet.

When I finally returned to the apartment building, it was well past midnight. The rain had stopped, leaving the streets slick and gleaming under the dim streetlights. I stood outside for a long time, staring up at the darkened windows, feeling the weight of everything that had happened pressing down on me. I didn't want to go back inside, didn't want to face the aftermath of what I had done, but there was nowhere else to go.

The elevator ride felt endless, the creaking of the old machinery filling the silence like an ominous soundtrack. When I reached my floor, the hallway was empty, the air thick with the smell of damp carpet and something else—something metallic and sharp that turned my stomach. I knew what it was before I reached her door.

Sylvie's apartment was exactly as I had left it. The door was ajar, the lights still on, casting long, eerie shadows across the walls. I pushed the door open with trembling hands, half-expecting to see her standing there, waiting for me with that knowing smile on her face.

But the apartment was empty. And in the center of the room, where I had left her, Sylvie lay motionless, her eyes staring blankly at the ceiling. The blood that had pooled around her had begun to dry, dark and sticky against the hardwood floor. The shard of glass was still embedded in her side, a twisted reminder of the violence that had ended everything.

For a moment, I couldn't move. I couldn't breathe. The reality of what I had done hit me all over again, harder than before, and I was paralyzed by the horror of it. I had killed her. I had taken a life. No matter what she had done to me, no matter how much she had twisted and manipulated me, I had been the one to end it. And now, there was no going back.

I forced myself to move, to turn away from the body, my vision blurring with tears. I couldn't stay here. I couldn't bear to be in this place any longer. I stumbled out of the apartment, leaving the door wide open behind me, and fled to my own unit.

When I reached my apartment, I slammed the door shut, leaning against it as if I could somehow block out the memories of what had just happened. The walls seemed to close in on me, the shadows stretching and twisting into familiar, haunting shapes. The whispers, once so loud and insistent, had fallen silent, but their absence was even more unsettling. The silence was thick, suffocating, like a blanket of ash smothering the remnants of my sanity.

I stumbled through the apartment, avoiding the mirrors, the windows—anything that might show me a reflection of the person I had become. My canvases were still there, half-finished and abandoned, but I couldn't bring myself to look at them. The urge to paint had been stripped away, leaving only emptiness in its place.

I collapsed onto the bed, curling up in a ball, and let the tears come. I cried for everything I had lost —my sense of self, my trust in my own mind, the future I had once dreamed of. I cried for Sylvie, for the person she had been before she became this monster, for the twisted bond we had shared. And I cried for the person I had become, the one who had been pushed so far that she had lost everything, even her humanity.

Hours passed in a blur of tears and exhaustion, until finally, I drifted into a fitful sleep. The nightmares were waiting for me, as they always were, but this time, they were different. Sylvie was there, as I knew she would be, but instead of tormenting me, she was silent, watching with a look of quiet satisfaction on her face. I tried to speak, to ask her why, but the words wouldn't come. She just stood there, smiling that cold, knowing smile, until I woke up with a start, drenched in sweat.

The apartment was dark, the first light of dawn just beginning to creep through the curtains. I sat up, the heaviness of the night still pressing down on me, but there was something else there too—something lighter, something that felt almost like clarity.

I had done terrible things, and I would have to live with the consequences for the rest of my life. But I had survived. Somehow, I had come through the other side, and that had to mean something.

I got out of bed, my movements slow and deliberate, and walked to the window. The sky was a pale gray, the city below still shrouded in early morning mist. For the first time in what felt like forever, I felt like I could breathe again.

But the relief was fleeting. As I stood there, staring out at the city, I felt a familiar chill creep up my spine. I turned away from the window, my gaze falling on the mirror above the dresser. The reflection was mine—tired, worn, haunted—but there was something else there, something I couldn't quite place. A shadow, a flicker, just at the edge of my vision.

I blinked, and it was gone, but the unease remained. I couldn't shake the feeling that I wasn't alone, that Sylvie's influence was still lingering, still watching.

I forced myself to turn away, to ignore the creeping dread. I had survived her once, and I could survive her again. But as I left the apartment, stepping out into the early morning light, I couldn't help but glance over my shoulder, just to be sure.

The building loomed behind me, dark and foreboding, its windows like empty eyes watching my every move. I walked away quickly, my footsteps echoing in the quiet street, trying to shake the feeling that I was still being followed, still being watched.

Even now, I can't be sure if it was real or just another trick of my mind. But as I walked through the city that morning, I couldn't help but feel that no matter how far I went, no matter what I did, Sylvie would always be there, lurking in the shadows of my mind, a reminder of everything I had lost, and everything I had become.

And maybe, just maybe, I wasn't as free as I thought.

9

## THE LINGERING SHADOW

The days had a strange way of blurring together after everything that happened. Weeks passed, and I tried to settle into a new routine, one that didn't involve looking over my shoulder or questioning every shadow. I moved across the city, far from that apartment building, to a smaller place in a quiet neighborhood where the streets were lined with trees and the only sounds at night were the occasional bark of a distant dog or the rustle of leaves in the wind.

It wasn't home, not yet. But it was safe. Or at least, it felt safe enough.

I hadn't painted since that night. The thought of picking up a brush, of pressing paint onto canvas, filled me with a deep, gnawing dread that I couldn't explain. The easel I'd set up in the corner of my new apartment sat empty, a silent reminder of the person I used to be, the person I wasn't sure I wanted to be again. I told myself it was okay to take a break, to let myself heal before diving back into something that had caused so much pain. But every day that passed without painting felt like another piece of me slipping away, another part of my identity that I couldn't get back.

I tried to fill the void with other things—reading, long walks through the city, even picking up a part-time job at a local bookstore. The people there were kind, patient with my quietness, my hesitation. They didn't ask questions, and I didn't offer any explanations. I just showed up, did my work, and left, grateful for the distraction, for the chance to be someone else for a few hours.

But no matter how hard I tried to move on, there was always something that pulled me back. A sound, a smell, a glimpse of something out of the corner of my eye that made my heart race, my breath catch in my throat. And at night, in the dark, when the world was quiet and still, I could feel her presence, just on the edge of my consciousness, like a shadow that wouldn't leave me alone.

I kept telling myself that it was just the trauma, the

aftershocks of everything I'd been through. But deep down, I knew it was more than that. Sylvie had left her mark on me, a scar that ran deeper than I wanted to admit. And no matter how far I ran, no matter how much distance I put between us, I couldn't shake the feeling that she was still there, lurking in the recesses of my mind.

It was on one of those long walks that I found myself back in the neighborhood where it all began. I hadn't planned to go there—hadn't even realized where I was until I turned a corner and saw the familiar shape of the apartment building rising above the trees. My heart skipped a beat, and I stopped in my tracks, staring up at the darkened windows.

It looked the same as it always had, a towering, ominous structure that seemed to swallow the light around it. I hadn't set foot near the place since that night, and just being this close made my skin crawl. But something compelled me to keep going, to take a few hesitant steps forward, until I was standing at the foot of the building, staring up at the window that used to be mine.

I don't know how long I stood there, lost in the memories that came flooding back, but eventually, I turned away, my chest tight with the weight of it all.

I had no reason to go back inside, no desire to revisit the place where everything had fallen apart. But as I started to walk away, something caught my eye—a small, unassuming art gallery tucked between two larger buildings, its window display filled with vibrant, abstract paintings.

I don't know why I walked in. Maybe I was searching for a connection to the part of me that I had left behind, the part that still longed to create, to paint. Or maybe it was something else, something deeper, more instinctual. Whatever it was, I found myself inside before I could stop myself, the familiar smell of oil paints and canvas filling my lungs.

The gallery was quiet, the only sound the soft hum of the overhead lights. I wandered through the space, my fingers trailing along the edges of the frames, my mind slowly beginning to ease as I took in the colors, the shapes, the raw emotion in each piece. For the first time in weeks, I felt something stir inside me, something that had been buried deep under layers of fear and doubt.

And then I saw it.

It was a small piece, tucked away in the corner of the gallery, almost easy to miss. But as soon as my eyes landed on it, my heart stopped. The colors, the brushstrokes, the unmistakable energy—it was Sylvie's work. I could recognize it anywhere. The painting was abstract, chaotic, but there was something familiar in the swirling darkness, something that made my skin prickle with recognition.

I stepped closer, my breath catching in my throat as I studied the piece. It was her, but it was more than that. It was us—our connection, our struggle, the push and pull of our twisted relationship, captured in every frantic stroke of the brush. It was as if she had taken everything that had happened between us and poured it into this one piece, leaving behind a part of herself that would never die.

A small, handwritten note was pinned to the wall beside the painting: *Untitled.* The artist's name was listed simply as "S."

My hands shook as I reached out to touch the edge of the frame, the wood smooth and cool beneath my fingertips. I didn't know what it meant, how it had gotten here, or what Sylvie had intended by leaving it behind. But as I stood there, staring at the twisted, haunting image, I felt a familiar chill creep up my spine.

She was still with me.

I could feel her, lurking in the shadows of the gallery, watching, waiting. A part of me wanted to run, to tear myself away from the painting and never look back. But another part of me—the part that had survived, that had fought so hard to break free—stood its ground.

"I'm not afraid of you," I whispered, the words barely audible, but they held a strength I hadn't felt in a long time.

The painting seemed to pulse with life, the darkness in the brushstrokes shifting, as if in response to my words. But I didn't flinch. I stood there, staring at it, refusing to let the fear take hold.

Finally, I turned and walked out of the gallery, leaving the painting behind, but I couldn't shake the feeling that it was still with me, that Sylvie was still with me, a shadow I would never fully escape.

As I stepped back into the light of the street, I took a deep breath, feeling the warmth of the sun on my face. I was free, but I knew that the freedom came with a price. Sylvie's influence had left a mark on me, one that would never fully fade. But I was still standing. I had survived. And for now, that was enough.

But as I walked away, a lingering doubt crept into my mind, a whisper that I couldn't quite ignore. Had I truly escaped her, or was this just another part of her game, another twist in the story she had begun?

I didn't have the answer. I wasn't sure I ever would. But as I moved forward into the unknown, I knew one thing for certain: Sylvie would always be a part of me, whether I liked it or not.

And maybe, just maybe, that was the most dangerous truth of all.